MY WEDDING DAY

STORY BY DEBORAH PACE ROWLEY ⁓ ILLUSTRATIONS BY GLENN HARMON

ISBN 13: 978-1-59955-016-9

Published by CFI, an imprint of Cedar Fort, Inc.
2373 W. 700 S., Springville, UT, 84663
Distributed by Cedar Fort, Inc., www.cedarfort.com

Jacket and book design by Nicole Williams
Cover design © 2007 by Lyle Mortimer
Printed on acid-free paper

Printed in China
10   9   8   7   6   5   4   3   2   1

DEDICATION

To my parents, who taught me by their example about eternal love.

D.R.

I would like to dedicate my work to my amazing wife. She has been my source of encouragement and support since the day I met her. I am so grateful to my Heavenly Father for the blessing to be married and sealed to her for all of eternity.

G.H.

Daddy, look at me. I'm the cutest wedding girl in the world. Are you going to walk me down the aisle?"

"I can't walk you down the aisle, sweetheart, but I'll do something even better. Come sit with me and I'll tell you a story. Imagine you are all grown up and it's your wedding day."

On your wedding day, Mommy will wake up early and bring you breakfast in bed with strawberries and whipped cream. She will climb on your bed, and you will whisper and laugh together because you will be so excited.

On your wedding day, you will come downstairs in your pajamas and sit in the old green chair. I'll give you a special father's blessing. When I'm done, I'll pull you close for a great big hug.

On your wedding day, I will carry your suitcase, your makeup bag, your wedding dress, your veil, your shoes, and your bouquet out to the car. The car will be so full that Mommy and I will get in and we will almost forget you.

 n your wedding day, we will drive to the most beautiful building in the world. It will look like a castle, sparkling and white in the sun. But it is better than a castle. It is a temple, the house of God, and you will have an invitation to go inside.

On your wedding day, we will walk into the temple, and Grandma will meet you in a special room just for brides. There will be mirrors and flowers and a chair just for you. It will be even more fun than playing dress-up. Grandma and Mommy will help you into a modest wedding dress and fuss over you until you look just right.

Then you will walk out of the bride's room and down the halls of the temple. You will be radiant with an inner light that will shine for everyone to see. That sparkle will come because you prepared for this day and kept yourself clean and worthy to marry in the House of the Lord.

On your wedding day, your family and friends will wait for you in a beautiful sealing room. Sunlight will shine through a stained glass window. A crystal chandelier will hang from the ceiling, and there will be an altar covered with lace.

You will walk into the sealing room, holding hands with the boy that you are going to marry. He will be dressed all in white, and he will be handsome—just like your dad. But even more important, he will be righteous and kind, and he will honor the priesthood of God. He will be excited, and his eyes will sparkle when he looks at you, just like my eyes do when I look at your mom.

On your wedding day, your future husband will lead you across the room, and you will kneel together at the altar. Then a sealer will give you wise counsel and perform the marriage ordinance. A sealer holds the priesthood power to seal husbands and wives together not just for this life, but for all eternity. I know if we keep our covenants, Mommy will be my wife forever, and I will always be your dad. God makes us this promise in the temple.

On your wedding day, Mommy will cry tears of joy. And I'll tell you a secret; your big, tough dad will cry too. Your husband will lean over and give you a kiss, and he won't believe how happy he feels because you are his wife.

Then you will stand with your new husband, and you will look into a mirror with a golden frame that hangs in the sealing room. The sealer will ask you what you see. You will see that your reflection goes on and on forever. This is because you have started an eternal family that never ends.

On your wedding day, you will walk out of the temple and into the flower gardens on the temple grounds. Photographers will take your picture, and it will be easy to get you to smile. Your heart will feel so happy that you will want to dance and jump up and down in your wedding dress. You will know that I love you. You will know that your husband loves you, and you will know that your Heavenly Father loves you.

On your wedding day, you will be the cutest wedding girl in the world, not because of your wedding dress or the fluffy veil or the pretty flowers in your hands. You will be the cutest wedding girl in the world because you are a daughter of God, because you are getting married in His house, and because you are mine.